The Adventures of Bob
Forest of Solitude

The Adventures of Bob
Forest of Solitude

Written & Illustrated By
Sahasrad Nalla

Disclaimer

This book has been published with all reasonable efforts taken to make the material error-free after the consent of the author. This book is sold subject to the condition that it shall not, by way of trade or otherwise, be lent, resold, or otherwise circulated without the copyright owner's prior written consent in any form of binding or cover other than that in which it is published and without a similar condition including this condition being imposed on the subsequent purchaser and without limiting the rights under copyright reserved above, no part of this publication maybe reproduced, stored in or introduced into a retrieval system or transmitted in any form or by any other means without the permission of the copyright owner.

Registered Office- 907-Sneh Nagar, Sapna Sangeeta Road,
Agrasen Square, Indore – 452001 (M.P.), India
Website: http://www.wingspublication.com
Email: mybook@wingspublication.com

First Published by WINGS PUBLICATION 2024
Copyright **Sahasrad Nalla** 2024

Title: **THE ADVENTURES OF BOB - FOREST OF SOLITUDE**
Price: Rs. 450 | $10 | AED 25
All Rights Reserved.
ISBN 978-93-6006-139-5

LIMITS OF LIABILITY/DISCLAIMER OF WARRANTY

The Author of this book is solely responsible and liable for its content including but not limited to the views, representations, descriptions, statements, information, opinions and references. The information presented in this book is solely compiled by the Author from sources believed to be accurate and the Publisher assumes no responsibility for any errors or omissions. The information is not intended to replace or substitute professional advice.

The Content of this book shall not constitute or be construed or deemed to reflect the opinion or expression of the Publisher. Publisher of this book does not endorse or approve any content of this book or guarantee the reliability, accuracy or completeness of the content published herein and do not make any representations or warranties of any kind, express or implied, including but not limited to the implied warranties of merchantability, fitness for a particular purpose. The Publisher shall not be held liable whatsoever for any errors, omissions, whether such errors or omissions result from negligence, accident, or any other cause or claims for loss or damages of any kind, including without limitation, indirect or consequential loss or damage arising out of use, inability to use, or about the reliability, accuracy or sufficiency of the information contained in this book. All disputes are subject to Indore (M.P.) jurisdiction only.

Acknowledgements

I am deeply grateful to my family whose unwavering support and understanding made this book possible. A special thank you to my mum for helping with the illustrations.

I am indebted to my parents and teachers for instilling in me a love for learning and storytelling. Your guidance and wisdom have shaped both this book and my journey as a writer.

Most importantly, to my brother, Abhiram, who provided support, encouragement, and a listening ear, thank you for believing in me and cheering me on throughout this endeavor.

All rights reserved. No part of this publication may be copied or reproduced without the prior permission of the copyright holder.

Table of Contents

- Chapter 1: The Hero
- Chapter 2: The Ancient City
- Chapter 3: The Dream
- Chapter 4: The Village
- Chapter 5: The Robbers
- Chapter 6: The Joyless Jungle
- Chapter 7: The Ghastly Glaciers
- Chapter 8: The Vicious Volcanoes
- Chapter 9: The Sad Swamps
- Chapter 10: The Treasure Cove

Chapter 1

Once upon a time, centuries ago, there was a boy named Bob and life was good. He had two loving parents who cared for him in every way as they worked hard to bring the bread-and-butter home, took care of him, taught him what was right and wrong, spent a lot of time playing and having fun with him. Although, in all that goodness and fun, there was something missing. Bob did not know what it was. Over time, he realized what it was. Life had become too boring and repetitive. He had heard of a perplexing and magical forest that had twists at every turn with a Treasure Cove at the end. Its name was the Forest of Solitude.

It was near the village, but his mum and dad would not let him go. The rumours suggested there were dangerous creatures and inexplainable horrors that lay in there. However, Bob did not believe those rumours based on absolutely nothing! He said to himself,

"How could anyone say anything if no one has ever been there and lived to tell the tale?"

Now he was more driven to go into the forest and come out victorious in order to prove the people wrong. There was no stopping him now. One night, Bob's parents had gone to bed and were sleeping quite soundly and deeply as they were exhausted after a full day's work. Bob went to bed and then, slept too.

He was somehow restless and woke up in the middle of the night. His parents were still sleeping and so, opportunity had struck.

Bob was able to pack food, water, a sword, some sticks, ropes, wool, a bow, and arrow all in a huge bag. Luckily, it was not as heavy as expected and plus, he was strong from lifting wood while helping his father.

Bob began his journey, determined to uncover and reveal the secrets in the **Forest of Solitude.**

Chapter 2

After some time cutting through vines and leaves, he found an ancient city hidden deep in the forest. He found a few artifacts and maps but other than that, nothing else. Determined, he kept moving forward and continued to explore. After a long while, he was thrilled to find a place that looked like the treasury, a place where the kings kept their gold. He realized this was a kingdom that had been abandoned for decades. There were claw marks on the walls and the reason the place was abandoned remained unknown. Little did **Bob** know that a deadly, HUGE MONSTER was lurking in the shadows...

Prowling through the darkness, disaster arrived.

As **Bob** headed towards the treasury carefully, the monster jumped out of the shadows and started to roar mightily. The very presence of it could make one tremble in fear.

Reminiscing his childhood stories, he knew the monster must be the infamous **Scorplox**.

He was a giant and powerful scorpion. However, Bob was brave and forged ahead.

"Get out of my way!" he said without hesitation.

"No, I will not!" said the monster angrily.

Both attacked each other with furious hits and blows. Trying to find a weak spot, Bob was carefully watching out for the monster's movements. He observed and realized that the only weakness that the scorpion had was its right arm. He assumed it was probably due to a past injury that never healed. Nevertheless, the scorpion was tough and precise, so he hit Bob hard. Bob practically flew to the wall and hurt himself severely. Wanting revenge, Bob, cold as ice, stepped forward and plunged his sword deep into the arm of the scorpion. It yelled in pain yet continued to fight. They were trading critical and crucial blows, each one leading them to the ultimate moments of the battle. After a strategic blow, the scorpion gave in and collapsed. Though Bob was weary and tired, he had a feeling of triumph and achievement. He managed to make himself a bed and slept soundly.

Chapter 3

Bob had a dream about an evil king saying to him, "If you stay in the Forest of Solitude, you will be captured, and further punishment will take place at the palace of doom."

He sounded profoundly serious and real, but Bob did not believe him and said "No!" The evil king then said angrily,

"Do not set foot in the forest again or else!" His words sounded like the truth, a solid threat!

Before Bob could say anything or ask any questions, he woke up in a fright. The morning went okay. No soldiers or guards came to take him away.

However, Bob was still tense and vigilant as well as worried about the night before.

To take his mind off things, he took a walk around the ancient city to see what else he could find. The only item which seemed useful was the treasure map he had found earlier.

As his eyes wandered around, he saw that the treasury had a lot of gold coins, rare gems and a shiny sword too. The sword looked exquisite and seemed to have been forged in a volcanic eruption using the purest of metals. Bob couldn't believe his luck! He took all of it and packed up his things and headed off towards his next glorious quest.

For his new quest, he decided that he should follow the treasure map and to discover what the treasure was. After seeing the map and the trail, he realized that the journey would be perilous and risky.

He would have to pass the Joyless Jungle, Ghastly Glaciers, Vicious Volcanoes, and Sad Swamps.

He would need a sidekick and a comrade and most importantly, a trustworthy friend who he could count on in order to watch his back and look out for him. He also mustn't be a backstabber and leave **Bob** for dead if things were to go awry. After thinking for some time, **Bob** remembered there was a village nearby and decided to check it out.

Chapter 4

When Bob found the village, it was night and he was tired. He soon found an inn and spent the night there. In the morning, he woke up, had his breakfast, and headed into the village to find a sidekick. While strolling around, he saw that there were wheat farms, the village's main food supply, which had crops that were growing fast under their care. After a prolonged observation, Bob thought to himself, "They must have professionals working on the farm."

This was true. The village was rich due to trading fresh wheat with neighboring villages. Expert farmers were born here too. So, in the faraway lands, they were the best village for farming. He also saw blacksmiths and they were forging swords and shields to put on for sale. Bob saw the quality of metals and the amount of effort that the workmen put in order to build top quality artillery. Bob strolled on, met a few villagers and chatted along. Most of them were farmers and blacksmiths but none of them were fighters or warriors.

One of them was Jeff and he seemed to be a nice guy. He was one of the only fighters in the village and he was a good one too. Bob chatted with Jeff and they went to a cook house together. They had a nice meal, and the chatting went on forever. They became friends rather spontaneously.

The day after that, Bob decided to ask Jeff to go on an adventure together. Without hesitation, the moment he saw Jeff, he asked nervously,

"Jeff, do you want to go on an adventure with me?"

Bob waited for the reply as Jeff stopped and thought about it for a moment. He responded saying,

"Yeah, I'd love to and could use a break from the village. So yes, I'll come with you"

Bob was elated and so the duo began their journey together.

Chapter 5

The next phase of the adventure began as **Bob** and Jeff started packing more food and weapons so that they would have enough supplies on the way. They could stop by places and get food too. They would also require an arsenal of weapons to choose from depending on the place and situation too. To ensure safety, **Bob** also kept a knife in his pocket. He said confidently,

> "Now, I'll always have a weapon. Just in case anything happens."

Meanwhile, as **Bob** was packing, Jeff was saying farewell and goodbye to his friends and family as he would be leaving for a long time. While Jeff was busy bidding farewell, Bob quipped,

> "Time to get ready with the armor and more."

Jeff said his final goodbyes and then hurried off with **Bob** to the inn.

As they were busily wearing armor, out of nowhere, robbers barged in and attacked. In the end, after a struggle, they had **Bob** and Jeff tied to poles. They stole the treasure **Bob** had found in the ancient city. Then the main gangster said tauntingly:

"Oh well! We have your gold and gems. There is nothing you can do!"

Bob suddenly remembered he had a knife in his pocket. He used the knife to cut the ropes while pretending that he was still tied up. The robbers, in the meantime, were discussing the best way to escape.

Swinging into action, **Bob** injured two of them in their legs and crushed the others using his strength. The leader, terrified of **Bob**'s brute strength, cowardly fled from the scene, leaving the gems and treasure behind.

Packing up their things and steadily recovering, **Bob** and Jeff set off on a path that would change their lives forever.

Chapter 6

Bob and Jeff were tense and restless thinking about their ordeal with the robbers. They were tormented by nightmares with visions of robbers stealing their precious treasure and hurting them. That left them traumatized and scared.

Overcoming their fears, they reached the Joyless Jungle. The trees were huge towers, and the thriving vines glowed as they wound themselves around the trees. When they were exploring and wandering round the diverse and naturistic surroundings, they found a kingdom, a flourishing kingdom. Moreover, it was not an abandoned one. It was surprisingly full of people.

However, they were not happy but instead, gloomy and sad. Bob questioned,

"Why are you all so sad? Is something wrong or is it something else?"

The people quickly responded saying:

"We always must deal with a creature known as Sonipon. It uses sonic booms to attack its prey. Every year it comes and steals our food. When it does, we are left with no food for months and have to nearly starve to death. We have no fighters or warriors to defend us, let alone vanquish the sonipon. PLEASE help us in our time of need!"

Bob couldn't imagine the pain and suffering the people were going through on that unfortunate day. Determined to save the people, Bob and Jeff made enquiries to understand more about the Sonipon. They quickly located the hideout of the deadly beast and hurried off to battle it. They fiercely fought the Sonipon though it was mighty and defensive. After some time, Bob managed to land a few hits of his own while Jeff distracted it, blocking and dodging the countless sonic booms it threw at him. They finally defeated the beast, and the kingdom was safe and sound again. The villagers were immensely thankful and happy. They renamed the jungle the "Joyful Jungle". Bob was happy and so was Jeff. They victoriously continued their journey to the Ghastly Glaciers.

Chapter 7

The Ghastly Glaciers was a terrifying sight to behold.

A fog was sweeping through the town and people were roaming the streets, some of them blinded by the dense cloud of mist. The talk of the town was that on certain days, people mysteriously disappeared into thin air!

Bob and Jeff, who considered themselves as heroes, pledging their duty to protect people, had to solve this mind-boggling mystery and find out the reason why people went missing on foggy nights.

They travelled to an inn, wanting to spend the night there. However, when they reached it, they were eager to find out the secrets of this mystery. So they questioned the person taking care of the place. Jeff asked:

"Why are people disappearing during the fogs and why isn't anyone trying to prevent it?"

The guy nervously responded:

"The reason that some people disappear during the fogs and never come back is unknown. No one can solve this and even the coppers do not know where they should start."

The villagers were scared and said:

"Please help us in our darkest hour! We beg you!"

Bob and Jeff pondered over what they had learnt from the villagers and started looking for clues to solve the mystery. They did some investigating and found out what it was. The village was haunted by a soul monster that stole souls of humans to enhance its powers.

Bob and Jeff meticulously prepared to capture the merciless beast. They successfully hatched a plan to attract the soul monster and bind it with shackles forever. They sought the help of villagers to build the strongest and largest casket in the world with a secret door within.

Bob took the brave step of acting as bait and laid in wait for the soul monster to come for its prey. As the beast unscrupulously entered the casket, looking to capture a soul, **Bob** instantly flipped the secret door to escape from the casket, while shutting it behind him with the strongest padlock made of iron. Simultaneously, Jeff along with the villagers shut the casket door to trap the soul monster inside.

Stunned and confused by the whole action, the soul monster bellowed in pain and anger. The crowd then carried the heavy casket and dumped it into the sea, far away from the village.

Peace, therefore, got restored in the Ghastly Glaciers. It then got renamed as the "Glorious Glaciers."

Triumphant, our heroes then continued their journey towards the Vicious Volcanoes.

Chapter 8

From the Glorious Glaciers, after a tiring, long journey, Bob and Jeff reached the Vicious Volcanoes.

When they reached the new place, they discovered a secret kingdom that was huge and hazardous. Its walls were made from hardened stone and believe it or not, there were LAVA PEOPLE!

Made from rocks and molten lava, with strength amounting to a thousand bulls, it was a species known as Lavados.

They lived near the two twin volcanoes known as Firefall and Ember Storm. They were still dormant, unlike most volcanoes in the area, waiting for their day to erupt. The lava people had the ability to mold lava into an item of their choice. Bob and Jeff were intrigued and interested in this fascinating ability and power. The amount of precision it took to execute this ability was boundless. They were bored and decided to go to the palace to ask if they could give out any quests that they could do in their own time.

Bob figured that this would be a pitstop, but Jeff wanted to conquer beasts and monsters. They argued about whether they should relax or fight epic battles with ferocious beasts. Finally, Bob caved in to Jeff's persuading. They went to the palace and asked,

"Do you have any quests for us?"

The lava king paused and thought for a moment and then started to whisper to his senior advisor. After some time, the king responded saying: "Yes, we do have a quest for you, but it is very risky and perilous. Should you choose to accept, if you are victorious, you shall be rewarded with a large amount of gold coins."

They accepted and the king explained the quest in more detail. They had to defeat a fire dragon that was eating away their life force, a rare slime of lava mixed with precious stones and crystals. Sadly, it also killed some of the king's men while they were protecting it.

They had to put an end to this.

Bob and Jeff headed to the cave where the dragon lived, equipped with armor, fire weaponry and precious stones. They devised a smart plan to conquer the beast and revive the king's men. Treading carefully and stealthily, they found the dragon in deep slumber. They took this as an opportunity and laid a trail of lava mixed with precious stones, leading the dragon towards a deep fire pit, an inescapable abyss.

The dragon woke up and seemed pleasantly surprised by what he saw. He mindlessly gathered the crystal slime and walked towards the pit.

Just when they thought their plan worked, the dragon realized that he had been tricked. Jumping into action, Bob and Jeff fired away at the dragon with their weapons.

The dragon slipped into the bottomless pit and was engulfed in the flames.

Soon thereafter, the cave glowed with light and small droplets of shiny crystals floated in the air.

POOOF!! The king's men were back, alive!

The king thanked Bob and Jeff profusely for their bravery and courage. They were awarded thousands of gold coins and an ancient manuscript called, the Way of the Wolf. The crowd cheered and the king renamed his kingdom the "Valorous Volcanoes."

The valiant heroes then set course for the Sad Swamps.

Chapter 9

When they reached there, they found a village filled with people who were sad and gloomy. All they did was work, work and work! They were also as still as a rock. It was almost as if someone sucked the happiness out of them and used it for something else.

Intrigued and confused, Bob and Jeff started to investigate. Tired after a long day and an arduous journey, they strolled around hoping to find a place to rest. Out of the blue, jumped a witch with a shiny wand and treacherous smile. She was muttering and mumbling something while using energy spells to try and suck the life out of them. She failed miserably as Bob and Jeff continued to dodge her endless spells. When she was done muttering gibberish, a giant pack of wolves arrived and attacked. It was clear that their minds were controlled by the witch who was using some sort of spell. Whatever it was, it also made them stronger, which made it harder for the duo to defeat. Bob thought to himself,

"Is the witch the reason for all the unhappiness in the village? Maybe she cast a spell?"

The witch was using the powers of happiness and positivity to strengthen her abilities. Of course, what could a witch want besides more power? Nothing! It was proven by the power she possessed.

Bob and Jeff climbed a house to escape from the wolves, hitting them along the way. However, the wolves, using their special powers, continued to climb the walls too. Amidst the chaos, Jeff realized the secret to the witch's powers. He said:

"It's the wand!! The wand is the place where she holds her power. So, technically, if we destroy the wand, the power she has will fade."

Bob had a think about this and said:

"It really is our best shot"

They made a couple of attempts but after some time, the witch realized what they were doing and stopped them. Bob threw his sword with all his might and miraculously, it worked!

The witch succumbed to her wounds and fled from the place, never to be seen again. Happiness was restored and the place was renamed the "Sunny Swamps."

Chapter 10

Having crossed all the dangerous places and perils, the duo realized that they had reached the end of the treasure route. Bob noticed it and told Jeff. There was still one last place to go to on the map.

It was a deep cave located near a ravine. When they reached it, they uncovered a maze of bewildering caves. They explored and walked through until they found something quite confusing. They noticed moss, the smell of fresh berries and felt cool breeze coming from inside the cave. As they cautiously walked inside, they discovered a lush and evergreen forest in the middle of the cave!! It was thriving and full of beautiful flowers, glowing plants and fruit-bearing trees. That is when it dawned on them.

They had reached the TREASURE COVE, the ultimate paradise of wealth, food and treasure.

Finally, **Bob** and **Jeff**, tired of battling monsters, dragons, beasts and witches realized they had reached their ultimate destination.

It was time to celebrate!!

They chatted and rested while talking about their adventures and wins. They also understood that life rewards those who are courageous, kind and perseverant.

The two friends packed their wealth and started their journey home, looking forward to new adventures in the future.

THE END

About the Author and Illustrator

Sahasrad Nalla, aged 10 years, loves reading books and is also a technology enthusiast. His love for reading and exploring started at a very young age. He started coding from the age of 6 and has developed Micro bit projects focused on supporting children to learn English alphabet the fun way while drawing in the air. He also successfully published his own HTML website through his school project.

Designing on Canva and discovering new possibilities is his hobby. The illustrations in this book were designed using Magic Media.

He hopes to leverage technology to build new innovations that help people around the world and successfully build his own company as an entrepreneur.

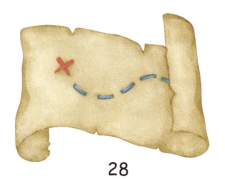

Milton Keynes UK
Ingram Content Group UK Ltd.
UKHW050230021224
451757UK00002B/14